Dear Parents:

Congratulations! Your child is taking the first steps on an exciting journey. The destination? Independent reading!

STEP INTO READING® will help your child get there. The program offers five steps to reading success. Each step includes fun stories and colorful art or photographs. In addition to original fiction and books with favorite characters, there are Step into Reading Non-Fiction Readers, Phonics Readers and Boxed Sets, Sticker Readers, and Comic Readers—a complete literacy program with something to interest every child.

Learning to Read, Step by Step!

Ready to Read   Preschool–Kindergarten
• big type and easy words • rhyme and rhythm • picture clues
For children who know the alphabet and are eager to begin reading.

Reading with Help   Preschool–Grade 1
• basic vocabulary • short sentences • simple stories
For children who recognize familiar words and sound out new words with help.

Reading on Your Own   Grades 1–3
• engaging characters • easy-to-follow plots • popular topics
For children who are ready to read on their own.

Reading Paragraphs   Grades 2–3
• challenging vocabulary • short paragraphs • exciting stories
For newly independent readers who read simple sentences with confidence.

Ready for Chapters   Grades 2–4
• chapters • longer paragraphs • full-color art
For children who want to take the plunge into chapter books but still like colorful pictures.

STEP INTO READING® is designed to give every child a successful reading experience. The grade levels are only guides; children will progress through the steps at their own speed, developing confidence in their reading.

Remember, a lifetime love of reading starts with a single step!

Step into Reading, Random House, and the Random House colophon are registered trademarks of Penguin Random House LLC.

Visit us on the Web!
StepIntoReading.com
rhcbooks.com

Educators and librarians, for a variety of teaching tools, visit us at RHTeachersLibrarians.com

ISBN 978-1-5247-6889-8 (trade) — ISBN 978-1-5247-6890-4 (lib. bdg.)

Printed in the United States of America   10 9 8 7 6 5 4 3 2 1

Nella
THE
PRINCESS
KNIGHT

I L♥VE King Dad!

based on the teleplay "A Striking Surprise"
by Jim Nolan

illustrated by Nneka Myers

Random House 🏠 New York

Nella and Norma
love to be with
their father.

Every day is
an adventure
with King Dad.

5

Sometimes they
go to the beach.

Catch the ball, Nella!

Sometimes they
have tea parties.

Norma eats a cookie.

<u>Yum!</u>

When King Dad's band
plays, they really rock!

Nella dances and dances.

Nella plays gobletball.
Her friends are
on her team.

King Dad cheers.

Hooray for Nella!

Nella also likes
to bowl with
King Dad.

Oh, no!
Some impkins
stop the game.
They take the
bowling balls!

The impkins roll

the balls everywhere!

Nella becomes a knight!

Her armor sparkles.

She shoots an arrow.
A ribbon is tied
to the arrow.

The ribbon stops
the rolling balls!

Nella saved the game!
King Dad hugs her.

When the day is over,
King Dad, Norma, and
Nella go home.

King Dad tucks
Norma into
her crib.

He reads Nella a story.

Nella loves King Dad!
And King Dad
loves Nella.